Timeless Fairy Tales

The Ugly Duckling

AWARD PUBLICATIONS LIMITED

It was summer, and all the fields and meadows were green. Mother Duck was sat on her nest in the pretty spot by the river bank, waiting.

She had been sitting on her eggs for a long time and she longed to go and swim in the cool river.

"I suppose they'll hatch soon," she thought.

A friendly old duck passed by to see if any of the eggs had hatched.

"Not yet," sighed Mother Duck, standing up just to check.

"Quack! Quack!" the old duck exclaimed. "I must say, that's a great big egg you have there." She peered closely at the egg. "It's twice the size of the others!"

Mother Duck patiently settled down again, and before long, to her great delight, the eggs began to crack, one by one. Soon she was the proud mother of six pretty yellow ducklings.

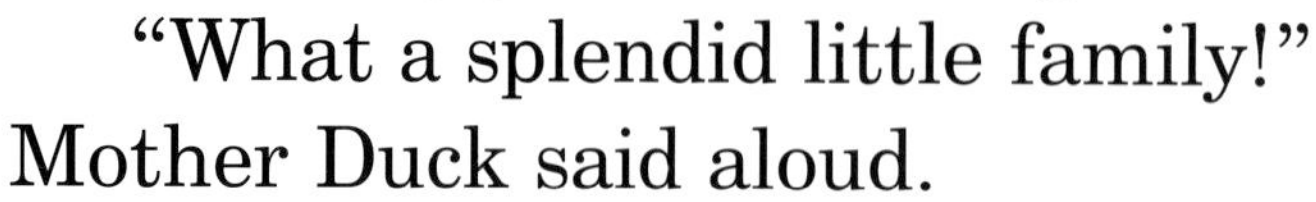

“What a splendid little family!” Mother Duck said aloud.

But the big egg was still unbroken, and so Mother Duck settled back down again.

When it finally cracked open, Mother Duck was amazed.

"Quack! Quack! Quack!" she cried, at the sight of her youngest. "You *are* a big bird!"

The youngest of her ducklings was so different from his brothers and sisters that Mother Duck just didn't know what to make of him.

The next day, Mother Duck set off for the river. Soon all her babies were swimming after her, and she could not help feeling pleased and proud. Even the big duckling swam just as well as his smaller brothers and sisters.

"That's a good thing," she said to herself. "He is a fine swimmer, so he must be a duck, after all."

After their swim, Mother Duck led the way to the farmyard to meet the other birds.

"You must all be very good," she warned. "Especially to Grandma Duck. She is the most important duck on the farm, so we need to behave nicely."

Unfortunately, the visit did not go well.

"I can't say I'm impressed," said Grandma Duck to Mother Duck.

"Six of your little ones are pretty enough, but that strange, ugly one doesn't belong here."

“That’s right, Grandma,” gobbled Turkey, interrupting her. “I’ve never seen such an odd duckling before…”

One of the hens prodded the poor duckling with her beak. He tried to creep under Mother Duck’s wing.

No one seemed to like the Ugly Duckling. Even the milkmaid shooed him out of her way whenever she passed.

None of his brothers and sisters wanted to play with him, either.

"You're much too big!" they all said.

The Ugly Duckling was so lonely and unhappy that he made up his mind to leave the farm. "Nobody will miss me," he told himself sadly, as he waddled away.

Eventually he reached the marsh where the wild ducks lived.

"Who are you? Where do you come from?" one of the wild ducks asked. "You are very odd!"

But the wild ducks weren't very interested in him, and soon flew away when some men with dogs and guns arrived.

One big, brown dog splashed through the water towards the Ugly Duckling, who was hiding in the rushes.

The big dog did not harm him, but the duckling was very frightened. "I'm going," he decided. "It's not safe here."

And off he went again.

As it began to get dark, the little duckling was too tired to go much further. He began to think about food and shelter for the night.

Then, in the moonlight, he saw a little house that looked very inviting. He began to think about food and shelter for the night.

"Maybe they'll let me stay here," he thought, as he went up to the door.

An old woman with a hen on her shoulder and a cat at her side opened the door and invited him inside.

"You are welcome to stay as long as you like," she said, "so long as you lay me an egg every day..."

But the Ugly Duckling could not lay eggs.

The old woman was so disappointed that she chased him out with her broom.

Her cat teased him and her hen pecked him.

"Why don't you go away?" they said. "We don't want you here."

So once again, the poor duckling found himself alone. No one wanted him.

The Ugly Duckling felt so sad and lonely that he didn't care where he went next.

He walked and walked, until at last he came to a lake. As soon as he was in the water, he swam and dived for water weeds, and began to feel better.

"I shall stay here for ever and ever," he decided. But soon the nights grew cold and the leaves on the trees changed to brown and yellow and then dropped to the hard earth.

Just before the first snowflakes fell, the duckling looked up into the wintry sky and saw some lovely white birds with long, graceful necks flying overhead. "Oh, how beautiful they are!" the Ugly Duckling cried. "If only I could look like them!"

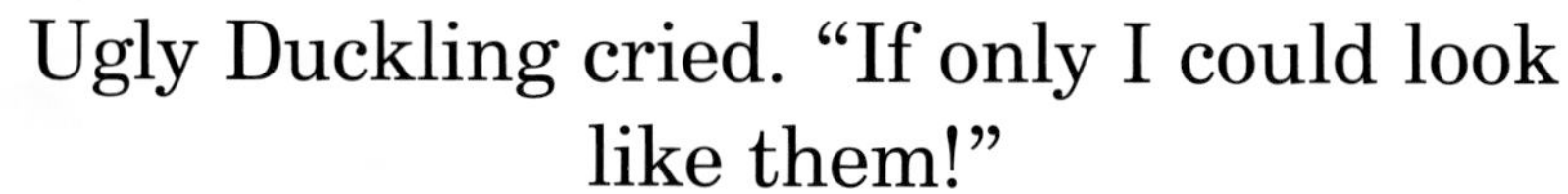

The duckling could not forget the beautiful birds, not even when an icy wind began to freeze the lake. Up and down he swam but the ice closed in all round him. One morning he found he was trapped in the ice and could not move.

He would have died if a young man had not come by. “Poor little chap,” he said. “I can’t leave you here to die!” And he broke the ice with his stout wooden clog.

Already very weak, the poor duckling had no strength to struggle.

“There!” said the man in a kindly voice. “I’ll carry you home under my jacket. It will shelter you from the bitter wind.”

The young man was poor but he was certain his wife would take care of the duckling until he grew stronger.

As soon as he got home, he called to his wife, and she picked up the duckling and held him gently.

"Of course we'll look after him," she said. "He can stay here with us until he is strong enough to fly."

In the warm farm kitchen, the Ugly Duckling soon began to recover.

The farmer's children were very excited to have a duckling in the house.

They wanted to play with him, but they were so noisy that the poor duckling was afraid of them.

He was so scared that he fled straight into the milk churn, knocking the milk all over the floor.

The mother was very cross with the children over the spilled milk. She tried to catch the frightened duckling, but, terrified, he crashed into the butter churn, knocking it over as well.

Desperately, the duckling looked for a way out of the house.

He slipped past the boy and made a frantic dash through the half-open kitchen door. Then he found himself outside. With a great effort, he used his remaining strength to escape across the snow-covered field.

Somehow he lived through the long, hard winter, making use of whatever shelter he could find.

One morning, in the warm spring sunshine, the Ugly Duckling felt a new strength in his wings. "Now I can really go into the wide, wide world," he told himself, as he rose into the air and flew away over the moors.

He came to rest in a pretty, scented garden, and there on the lake were some beautiful white swans!

The Ugly Duckling was filled with joy at the sight of them. “Even if they attack me because I am so ugly,” he thought, “what does it matter?” And he flew down on to the lake and swam towards the stately birds.

“Please don’t send me away!” cried the duckling, bending his head.

And then, the Ugly Duckling saw himself reflected in the clear water. Something strange and wonderful had happened! To his great surprise, he saw that he was no longer the ugly, grey bird that nobody loved, but a graceful, beautiful white swan, just like the others!

Some children came to the lake to feed the swans and they began throwing bread into the water. The girl cried, “Look! A new swan! And it’s the most beautiful of all!”

THE END